DORY the Rascal is gett

Should she bring . . .

A. Her imagination?

Bok! Bok!

Bok!

No way.

B. Her Santa hat?

C. The monster who
sleeps under her bed?

RRRING!

D. Her banana phone
in case of emergencies?

Will they help her find
a real true friend?

DORY
FANTASMAGORY

The Real True Friend

abby hanlon

PUFFIN BOOKS

To my collaborators

Louisiana Burke

PUFFIN BOOKS
An imprint of Penguin Random House LLC
375 Hudson Street
New York, New York 10014

First published in the United States of America by Dial Books for Young Readers,
an imprint of Penguin Group (USA) LLC, 2015
Published by Puffin Books, an imprint of Penguin Random House LLC, 2016

THE LIBRARY OF CONGRESS HAS CATALOGED THE DIAL BOOKS EDITION AS FOLLOWS:
Hanlon, Abby, author, illustrator.
Dory and the real true friend / by Abby Hanlon.
p. cm.
Summary: Dory, a highly imaginative youngest child, makes a new friend at school but her
brother and sister are sure Rosabelle is imaginary, just like all of Dory's other friends.
ISBN 978-0-525-42866-4 (hardcover)
[1. Imagination—Fiction. 2. Imaginary playmates—Fiction. 3. Schools—Fiction.
4. Friendship—Fiction. 5. Brothers and sisters—Fiction. 6. Family life—Fiction.] I. Title.
PZ7.H196359Dm 2015
[E]—dc23 2014034036

Puffin Books ISBN 9780147510686

Printed in the United States of America

7 9 10 8 6

Designed by Jennifer Kelly

A REAL TRUE FRIEND

An actual kid everyone can see
but who wants to play with you anyway

Wait a minute.
What about me?
Where did this come
from? This is not
the definition.

Mary

Mr. Nuggy

ME

CHAPTER 1
Such a Weirdo

My name is Dory, but everyone calls me Rascal. This is my family.

I have a mom, dad, big brother, and big sister who are just regular people. I also have a monster and fairy godmother who are not regular because only I can see them.

Mary is my monster. She sleeps under my bed and plays with me all day. Mr. Nuggy is my fairy godmother. He lives in the woods but comes over if I have an emergency. And I'm about to have an emergency pretty soon because . . .

. . . tomorrow is the first day of school!

I tell Mary the big news while we are playing our favorite game, exercise club.

"Oh yeah. Oh yeah. That place! With the water fountains!" says Mary. "There are so many kids and not a lot of grown-ups! Yippee! I love that place!" she says. "Let's get packing!"

Mary decides to make
a list of what I should
bring.

"I'm sorry, but I *cannot* read this," I say.

So she reads it to me. "Please bring to school tomorrow: Your dad's dirty laundry, extra salami, and lemon juice."

"*What a weird list!*" I say. "Are you *sure* you remember what
school is?"

"Uh-huh. Super
sure," she says.

"All right," I say.
"I'm trusting you."

First, we collect as much of my dad's dirty laundry as we can.

Then I stuff the laundry
in my backpack. It makes
me look like a big kid with
a backpack full of home-
work. *So that's what it's for!*

Second, we sneak down to the kitchen.
Luckily, no one is there. I grab a handful of
salami and put it in my lunch box. It's true,
my mom never packs me enough salami!

Third, we look for
the lemon juice.

"Okay. Let's figure out what this
is for," I tell Mary. "I'm gonna
take a tiny squeeze, and you
tell me what happens."
WOW! OOOO-YA!

"So?" I ask.

"Your muscles are HUGE!" says Mary.

"What else?" I say.

"And your bones are lit up like lightbulbs!"

"What else?"

"And you have magic eyebrows!" says Mary.

I don't know what that means, but I like it.

"Let's pack it!" I say.

Just then my brother and sister come in the kitchen.

"What are you doing?" asks my sister, Violet.

"Nothing," I say, while Mary quickly sneaks the bottle of lemon juice into my lunch box.

"You know, Rascal, you're going to have to get *dressed* for school! You can't wear that dirty old nightgown every day anymore," says Violet.

"And you can't talk to yourself at school," says my brother, Luke.

"And do not move the furniture around in your classroom to build a fort like you did last year," says Violet.

"Just try not to imagine things!" says Luke. "That's ALL you have to remember, Rascal."

"Right," says Violet, pointing her finger. "No matter what, do NOT use your imagination!"

". . . like telling people that monsters live in our house!" says Luke.

". . . or talking about Mrs. Gobble Gracker!" says Violet.

"*Mrs. Who?* I'm done with her!" I say, which is a huge lie because Mrs. Gobble Gracker is still my favorite game.

Mrs. Gobble Gracker is a robber, and she is five hundred and seven years old, and she has very sharp teeth, and she wanted to steal me away from my family and lock me in her cave forever, but I was too tricky.

"And," says Violet, "the most important thing for you to remember is, DON'T BE YOURSELF. Can you do that?"

"Rascal? What are you staring at?" says Luke. "Pay attention!"

"Do you know why we are telling you all this?" says Violet, shaking my shoulders. "Wake up! Pay attention!

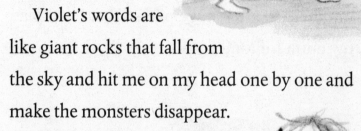

"BECAUSE!! IF YOU
ACT LIKE SUCH A
WEIRDO, NOBODY
WILL WANT TO BE
FRIENDS WITH YOU."

Violet's words are
like giant rocks that fall from
the sky and hit me on my head one by one and
make the monsters disappear.

"What?" I say.

Violet says slowly, "Because.
You. Won't. Have. Any. Friends."

"I don't care," I say. But I
imagine myself all alone at recess.

"If you want friends," says
Violet, "you should listen to me. You should
plan your outfit for the first day of school."

"I'm busy already," I say, walking backward out of the kitchen. Then I turn around and run upstairs to my room and shut the door.

As fast as I can, I take all of my clothes out of my drawers, every single one of them, and put them in a big huge pile so that I can plan my outfit for tomorrow.

I search for all my best clothes to wear on the first day of school.

These plaid pants

 This polka-dotted shirt

This... rainbow shirt on top

 striped socks

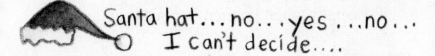 Santa hat...no...yes...no... I can't decide....

"Definitely wear the hat!" says Mary.
"That's what I thought," I say.

She looks amazing.

"But what am *I* going to wear to school?" asks Mary.

Last year, I brought Mary to school with me every day. But now I think she'd better stay home. Especially when I remember last year . . .

LAST YEAR:

Mary always said she had to go to the bathroom, when she really didn't have to go. She just wanted to play with the soap in the bathroom. So one day the teacher said NO she couldn't go. But guess what? She really did have to go! So do you know what happened? ... *All over the floor.*

Also, it turned out that Mary was hiding salami in her desk.

Oh yeah, and one day she took her shoes off and then she couldn't find them. . . . Nobody *ever* found them. I felt so bad for her that I let her borrow my shoes.

She also whispered
bathroom words in
everybody's ears.

And she could never remember to raise her hand. She interrupted all the time. And her answer for everything was "chicken!"

"Sorry, Mary, you have to stay home," I tell her. "Last year was too crazy!"

Mary sulks. "But without me, you won't have a friend."

"I'm going to make a new friend," I say. "A *real* friend."

"NOOOOOOOO!!!" says Mary, bursting into tears, "Pleeeeease, no!!!"

That night my brain keeps waking me up with so many questions.

Who will I play with at recess?

Will I be lonely without Mary?

Will I miss my nightgown?

Am I such a weirdo?

Are we going to have a class pet?

Could it be a hamster?

Could we name it Flowerball?

Are we going to have Opposite Day?

Will I wear my clothes inside out AND backward for Opposite Day?

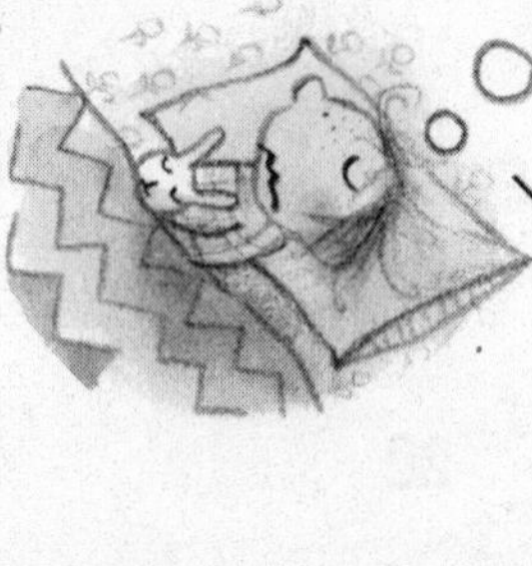

What will my teacher look like?

I wake up my dad
and tell him I have a
stomachache.

He says, "You don't really have a stomachache." And I say, "But how do you know?" And
he says, "Because the other night you told me
you had a stomachache in your ear."

"So?" I say.

"Good night!" he says.

But I still can't sleep, so I call Mr. Nuggy.

Whoa,
that was fast.

"I'm scared about school," I say. "I don't want to go. You've got to help me. What can you do? Can you use your magic wand to make it go away?"

"Don't worry," he says. "I have a plan. I'm going to do some magic and turn your whole school into a pancake, so you won't have to go, ever."

"A pancake?" I ask.

"Yes, but it's a very complicated recipe, and I'm going to need some chickens, and it might take a few days."

"All right, that's okay," I say.

A pancake sounds just fine, I think. *A great big giant buttery pancake instead of school would be perfect* is my last thought before I close my eyes and finally fall asleep.

CHAPTER 2
Best Friends Forever

When I come down for breakfast, Violet bursts out laughing. "Mom! Rascal is wearing the exact same outfit she wore every day last year! And now it's way too small for her!"

My mom says, "Oh, she can wear what she wants. It's not a big deal."

"The Santa hat isn't too small," I say.

"But it's a Santa hat!" yells Violet.

While I'm eating breakfast, my mom sits

down with me and says she has some important reminders about school.

1. "Don't move the chairs and desks around the room."

"I ALREADY KNOW ABOUT THAT!" I yell.

"Okay, okay, calm down!" she says.

2. "Keep your shoes on."

"Why would I take my shoes off?"

"I don't know, Dory. I still don't understand how you lost so many shoes last year."

3. "Absolutely no bathroom words! Do you understand me, Dory? I mean it. Save them for home, when you are in the bathroom, all by yourself, with the door shut."

"BOR–ING!" I say.

"I think you are going to have a super day," says my mom. "I'll miss you."

As we leave for school, Luke says, "We are
not walking with you if you wear that hat."

"Oh, fine," I grumble.

When we get to school, Violet walks me to my classroom door. I grab on tightly to her. I wish I were home in my nightgown.

"Don't leave me here," I say. But she is already walking away.

The teacher meets me at the door and says, "Let's hang up that *huge* backpack," and she walks me to the closet, smiling. I immediately fall in love with the closet.

It's sooooooo long! It has six doors! There are no cubbies like last year, so you can crawl

around. I hang up my backpack on a hook. I want to sneak right into that dark cozy space behind all the backpacks, but the teacher is standing there waiting for me.

"Now let's find your table," she says.

There is somebody at my table who is stuck in a shirt.

I look around for the teacher to help, but she is already helping someone else.

Oh dear. I'm going to have to do this. I pull really hard on his shirt, and pull and pull and pull, and off it comes! *It's George!* George was in my class last year. "Thanks," he says, and then he falls off his chair.

When he gets up, he asks me, "Where's Mary? Did you bring her?"

"No," I say, embarrassed that he remembers.

"Aw shucks!" he says. "She was so funny. I liked when she moved all the furniture around."

I pretend that I have no idea what he is talking about.

The teacher gives us markers and tells us to draw self-portraits. I draw myself as a dog named Chickenbone. I give myself an eye patch, just 'cause. George draws himself with a bunch of creepy scars on his face.

I peek at the drawing of the girl sitting next to me. What???? OH MY!

She drew earrings! And earlobes! And curly eyelashes! And nostrils!! And a crown—covered in jewels!

When I look at her, she smiles at me, oh my . . . Holy Cow! I don't believe it . . . *SHE IS MISSING HER TWO FRONT TEETH!!!*

I decide at that very moment that she is my best friend.

She is wearing an old-fashioned dress that looks especially poufy. She has sparkly shoes with little tiny heels. She wore heels! *To school!* She smells like bubble bath, and she even has circle earrings that I think she drew on with a green marker. And I don't know why, but she is wearing her headband on her forehead instead of her head.

I decide to whisper something funny to her. "Do you know what happens if you don't put the tops back on Magic Markers?" I say. She shakes her head no.

"They EXPLODE! *POW! BOOM! WHAM!*" I say.

I thought she was going to laugh, but instead she looks worried and quickly puts all the tops back on the markers.

But George gets excited by this and he explodes—"POW! BOOM! WHAM!"—and falls out of his chair again.

"That was fun," says George, lying on the floor, looking dizzy. That's what he always says when he gets hurt. Even if he is crying, he still says it. Then he leans forward and points to the girl. "Your forehead is falling down!" he says to her.

"What?" she says, grabbing on to her forehead.

"He means your headband," I say.

"It's not a headband," she says, and keeps drawing.

And then I hear her mumble in a very quiet whisper, "It's a crown."

George and I look at each other, confused.

At story time
on the rug, I rush
to get a seat next
to her.

The teacher says to her, "Rosabelle, move over a little please."

ROSABELLE? Did she say Rosabelle?? That is the most beautiful name *I have ever heard in my entire life. Rosabelle, Rosabelle, Rosabelle* I say in my head over and over again.

At lunchtime, I sit next to Rosabelle and George sits next to me. We watch in amazement as Rosabelle opens her lunch box, and takes out first a flowered place mat and matching cloth napkin (which she places on her lap), then a matching china cup and saucer. Then she takes out her water bottle and pours water into the cup and takes a little sip with her pinkie sticking up in the air like this:

Then she takes out a peanut butter and jelly sandwich and cuts it up with a knife and takes bites with a fork, while wiping her face with the napkin after each bite. I am so busy watching Rosabelle eat that I barely have time to eat my salami.

When it's finally recess, I get my first chance to be alone with Rosabelle.

"How did you get so poufy?" I ask Rosabelle, pointing to her dress.

She looks down and says, "It's a secret, but I'll show you."

Underneath her dress, she has six different skirts on. She shows me each one. And for each one, I say, "Wow!"

1. One flower skirt

2. One plaid skirt

3. One strawberry skirt

4. One polka-dotted skirt

5. One palm tree skirt

6. One very ruffly  skirt

"Guess what?" I say. "I have a secret, too."

"You do? What is it?" she asks.

I'm trying to think of a secret. . . . I'm sure I have one. . . . I usually do.

I unzip my lunch box and take out the lemon juice. "It's a magical liquid. Do you know what happens if you squeeze it into your mouth? You get very strong and you can fight bullies!"

Rosabelle looks really surprised.

"Are there bullies???" she asks. "Are they dangerous?"

"I don't know yet . . . but watch me try it. . . ." I squeeze some in my mouth, but I get WAY too much, a huge enormous gulp. It's SOOO sour, I can't help but make a *really crazy face*, and I start choking and gagging.

"Are you all right?" she asks.

I nod my head yes, but I'm still gagging.

Just then some girls run toward us, giggling
and screaming, saying, "Rosabelle! Hopscotch!
Hopscotch!" And they
pull her away.

In the afternoon, we have choice time. When everyone is busy, I sneak into the closet for a super-quick bite of salami.

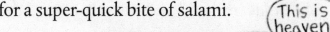

It's so good that I stuff some salami in my pockets, so I can share with Rosabelle.

"Here . . . look, do you want some floppy cookies?" I whisper to her, which is my nick-name for salami because I love it so much.

She does not.

After school, we line up to wait for our parents. My mom comes first.

She holds my hand and we walk toward the school yard gate. But a few steps away, I realize, I just have to tell Rosabelle. *I just have to.*

"BEST FRIENDS FOREVER!!!" I shout, jumping up and down.

She smiles.

My mom says to me, "Really? You have a best friend already?"

"Yes, I do! I do! A real true friend!"

"What is her name?"

"Um???"

Oh gosh . . . *what was her name?* Something beautiful, but I JUST forgot it. Was it Annabelle? Rosebud? Roseblossom?

"Oh, I don't remember," I say. "What's my best friend's name again?"

CHAPTER 3
Chicken Soup

By the time I get home from school, Rosabelle's name has popped right back into my head. This time it stays forever.

"Did you hear about my best friend Rosabelle?" I ask Luke and Violet.

"About ten times already," says Violet.

"Well, she's extremely poufy. And she doesn't have a lot of teeth. And she wears a crown!"

"Not another monster!" says Luke.

"Forget it," I say angrily.

I wait until he walks away and then I jump on top of him.

"Rascal!" he yells, but then laughs . . . because it was such a good surprise attack.

And then we wrestle, and then he drags me around on the floor . . . my favorite.

When Luke gets bored playing with me, I go upstairs to my room. I open the door and I am shocked. The floor is covered in paper. It looks like Mary's been making rows and rows of letters *all day*.

"I'm practicing the alphabet! Look at these *s*'s! See how good I would be at school? Don't you think you should bring me?" she says, holding up pages and pages of *s*'s.

"I love my *s*'s so much, I'm going to save them to show my children one day."

"I'm not sure . . . ," I tell her, "but I think those *s*'s are all backward."

She falls over in disappointment.

"Come on, get up," I say. "Stop moping around. What else happened today while I was gone?"

"I played school with all the monsters. I was the teacher!"

"No wonder it's such a mess in here," I say. "They listened to you?" I ask her.

"Mostly," she says.

"Okay, what else happened?" I ask her.

"Mr. Nuggy called lots of times," she says.

"*Mr. Nuggy called me?* That's not how it's supposed to go! I'm supposed to call him! He's MY fairy godmother," I say.

"Well, he said he had an emergency."

"What kind of emergency could he have? *I'm the one with emergencies!*"

"I don't know, I couldn't understand him. He was bokking."

"*Bokking?* What the heck does that mean?"

Bokking?

"And it sounded like bokking from a cave or something. There was an echo."

"A *cave??*" Why would he be in a cave? "Quick, give me a banana."

"It's ringing. . . . Shh. . . . Hello?"

"*DoryDoryDory . . . ,*" says an evil voice. "I knew you would call." I'd recognize that voice anywhere.

"Mrs. Gobble Gracker?! Why do you have Mr. Nuggy's phone? Where is he?" I shout.

"Well . . . I ran into him in the woods the other day. He was trying to do some magic helping YOU, I guess, but he accidentally turned himself into a chicken. Now he's stuck. YOU KNOW how that happens. Well, I have some water boiling . . . it is getting to be dinnertime, and YOU KNOW how much I love soup . . . chicken soup."

"Mr. Nuggy is a chicken?" I scream into the phone.

"OH NOOOOOO! HE'S NEVER GOING TO BE ABLE TO TURN MY SCHOOL INTO A PANCAKE NOW! *DON'T EAT MY FAIRY GODMOTHER!*"

"What are you doing?" Violet suddenly appears in my doorway. "Please tell me you aren't playing *Mrs. Gobble Gracker*," she says.

"I'm in the middle of an important call," I tell Violet in my dead serious voice.

"Okay, fine," she says, turning away. "I guess you don't want to talk about school . . . or Rosabelle."

"Wait, I do," I say, and drop the banana.

"So, did you play with Rosabelle at recess?" she asks.

"Uh-huh," I say, even though it's not true. "It was really fun."

"What did you guys play?" she asks.

"We played . . . um . . . Mermaid . . . Puppies," I say the first two words that pop into my head.

"Mermaid Puppies . . ." she says. "Huh."

Maybe Violet has a feeling that I'm not telling the truth, because then she says, "You should plan your outfit for tomorrow. Wear something that Rosabelle will like."

"Okay, good idea," I say.

As soon as Violet leaves, I pick up the banana again. This time I whisper. "Hello, are you still there? Sorry to keep you waiting."

"It was very rude," says Mrs. Gobble Gracker.

"I'm sorry, I couldn't help it."

"What are Mermaid Puppies?" she asks.

"What? You could hear that? I don't know what Mermaid Puppies are! That's not the point of this conversation! Listen, please don't eat Mr. Nuggy. I beg you. I'll give you anything. Just tell me, *what do you want?*"

"I'll think about it," she says. "I'll let you know."

"*When?*" I say. "I need to know when!"

But she has already hung up.

Without Mr. Nuggy, I'm on my own. And now Mary is so jealous of Rosabelle, she is having a fit.

So I have nothing left to do but wait for Mrs. Gobble Gracker to call back. And plan my outfit...

9 pairs of underwear

3 pairs of leggings

4 shirts

3 pairs of socks

CHAPTER 4
Get Out of the Sticky Frogs!

The next morning, I wake up early because I need time to put on my outfit.

When I come down for breakfast, Violet says, "Why do you look weird?"

"No, I don't," I say, deciding it would be better not to tell her.

"You look . . . all bunchy," she says.

"And your butt looks big," says Luke.

"And you're sweating," says Violet.

"I don't know what you are talking about," I lie.

When I get to school, I tell Rosabelle, "Just wait till recess, I have a new secret for you."

"Is it recess yet?" I ask my teacher.

"No, honey," she says. "We just got here. Come to the rug for circle time."

During circle time, I have to wait forever and forever for my turn to speak. *Everyone in this class has something to say!*

I wait and wait for my turn to speak, and while I'm waiting I'm imagining that all the kids on the rug are newborn hamsters.

I snap out of it when it's Rosabelle's turn.

"Your stuffed animal?" says the teacher. "How cute."

"NO," says Rosabelle, shaking her head with a frown and then staring at the teacher as if the teacher is totally crazy. After a long silence, she says, "He flew into a hedge of thorns trying to save me."

Dragon??? Hedge of thorns? What is she talking about??

"Oh? Okay," says the teacher. "Very cute. Moving on . . . Dory, what did you want to say?"

"Um . . . um . . . ," *Of course, now I forgot.*

"That's okay, just tell us when you remember," says the teacher.

But there is no way I am going to lose my turn to speak! So I say the first thing I can think of. "I have a great game we could play today!"

"Can we pretend that all the kids are baby hamsters and you are trying to catch us and put us in a suitcase?"

My teacher says, "Uhhhh. . . . That sounds like a very fun game you could play at recess today, Dory."

"Well, if Rosabelle wants to . . . ," I say, looking at her.

But she doesn't look like she wants to.

The teacher smiles and says, "Does anybody
else have something to share this morning?"

George raises his hand and says, "I would
like to be a baby hamster named Marvin."

At lunch I can barely talk to Rosabelle because George won't stop talking about the hamster game. "Let's be hamsters with really bad manners! And we eat garbage! And we are hiding from the police! The police want to

capture all the hamsters and sell us to make hamster burgers! Raise your hand if you hate hamster burgers!" George says raising his hand.

"Gross!" I say, but it does sound kind of fun.

Finally it's recess.

"Ready for my secret?" I say to Rosabelle. I show her my nine pairs of underwear, three pairs of leggings, four shirts, and three pairs of socks.

"Now we are like twins!" I say. "We both have secret clothes!"

"Hmmm . . . ," she says, studying me carefully. "So you're padded. . . . Is it for protection? Is it like armor?"

I don't know how to answer that. "Well, it could be."

"Rosabelle! Come on!" The hopscotch girls are calling again.

"They were in my class last year," she says to me before they pull her away.

I take off three sweaty shirts. Then I follow her to the hopscotch game.

"Be careful!" I yell. "That square is full of dead sharks! Don't jump on the dead sharks!"

Rosabelle jumps to the next square. "Holy moly! Now you are stepping in sticky frogs! *Get out of the sticky frogs!*" Rosabelle loses her balance and lands in another square.

"AHHH!! Bubbling hot lava!! Jump out! Jump out! Quick!" I yell.

All the girls stop and look at me.

They keep looking at me.

"Do you want to play?" one of the girls asks me.

"Not really," I say. And I run away.

I wander around the school yard and watch what everyone else is playing.

There are girls galloping like horses.

There are kids playing house, but their house burned down and now they are all fighting.

George and some kids are playing hamsters.

Mary is doing her exercises.

Mary???!! What is she doing here?? I stomp over to her. "What are you doing here?" I ask angrily.

"Don't you want to exercise?" she says.

"Okay, just this once," I say. "But then go home!"

CHAPTER 5
Ring, Ring, Ring!

That afternoon, we have drawing time. Instead of starting my picture, I watch what Rosabelle draws. A big huge scaly dragon.

"Do you really have a dragon?" I ask her.

"Of course, I do," she says. "He's such a baby, though, and he always gets hurt. He even bumps into walls in the castle."

"You live in a castle?" I ask her.

"Where else would I live?" she asks. "Although I do have a little cottage in the woods when I need to hide."

"Do you have an underground base? I do!" says George. "Raise your hand if you have an underground hamster base!" he says, raising his hand.

I ignore George and ask Rosabelle, *"Hide from what?"*

"You know… creepy old witches, that kind of thing," says Rosabelle.

"Dory, aren't you going to draw something?"
asks the teacher, looking at my blank paper.
"Dory," she says, "can you hear me?

"Dory . . . ? Are you
there, Dory . . . ?"

After school, I rush straight to my room to get all my layers off and put my nightgown on and find out if I got any phone calls while I was gone.

Nobody called you.

"*She didn't call yet?*" I say. "Ugh! And I already told you! You don't have to raise your hand at home!"

Mary wants to come to school with me so

badly that she's been raising her hand when-
ever she wants to speak.

All afternoon, she won't stop practicing for
school.

She is quiet in the hallways.

She even waits in line for the bathroom.

Since Mary is driving me crazy, I'm happy when Luke and Violet finally come home from their friend's house.

"Guess what? I have *BIG HUMONGOUS NEWS!*" I tell them. "Rosabelle has a dragon! And she lives in a castle! I'm dead serious."

"See," Luke says to Violet. "I told you Rascal made Rosabelle up."

"What? I did not make her up! She is a real girl in my class! She sits next to me!"

"Is she real in the same way Mary is real?" asks Violet.

"Yes!" I say.

Mary smiles proudly.

"What does your teacher say when you talk to Rosabelle at school?" asks Luke.

"She says, '*Girls, please be quiet!*'"

Luke laughs at this.

"Do you play with anyone else at recess besides Rosabelle?" asks Violet.

"Well, I only play with Rosabelle sort of because she mostly likes to play hopscotch," I admit.

"Your imaginary friend doesn't even want to play with you!" Luke bursts out laughing again.

"I ALREADY TOLD YOU!!! ROSABELLE IS NOT IMAGINARY!!!!" I scream at the top of my lungs.

As I stomp out of the room in tears, Luke and Violet are still laughing. I hear Violet say, "Well, she told me they play *Mermaid Puppies*." Then I hear a loud thud. Luke must have laughed so hard he rolled off the couch. Like *Mermaid Puppies* is the funniest thing they've ever heard in their life.

I cry so hard that my whole room fills up with tears. Why are Luke and Violet such jerks? And what is so great about hopscotch? Will Rosabelle ever play with me? And where is Mr. Nuggy when I need him most?

"Maybe Rosabelle isn't my real true friend after all," I cry to Mary. "Maybe I'll never have a friend. Maybe Luke and Violet are right."

Mary pets my head while I cry.

"You can come to school with me tomorrow," I say, sobbing and sniffling.

"No thanks," she says.

"*WHAT?*" I say.

"I think I like *playing* school better than actually going."

"Ma-rrrrry! After all that begging? Errrr. But I need you now. I have no one to play with," I cry.

"I bet tomorrow Rosabelle will play with you," she says.

"How do you know?" I ask.

"*Just be yourself,*" she says.

So that's what I do.

The next day at lunch, I sit next to Rosa-belle. It's not easy to get a seat next to her, with the hopscotch girls around.

I open my lunch box and I AM SHOCKED to discover that my mom packed *my phone*!! Why would she pack my phone? *What was she thinking?* Oh my goodness, *WHAT IF IT RINGS?*

Please please *please*
don't let it ring.

Uh-oh.

RRINNG RRRING RRING RRING!

I have to answer it.
If I don't answer it, Mr.
Nuggy will be chicken soup.

"Hello?"

"Dory, how are you?" asks Mrs. Gobble
Gracker.

"Fine," I say, looking around the noisy cafeteria. I have to cover the other ear so I can hear her.

"I've decided what I want," she says.

"It's about time!"

"I will free Mr. Nuggy if you can get me what I want."

"Yes, anything," I say.

"I want a princess."

"A *princess*? Where am I going to get a . . ." And then I look over at Rosabelle, cutting her grapes in half and eating them with a fork.

I do some quick math in my head.

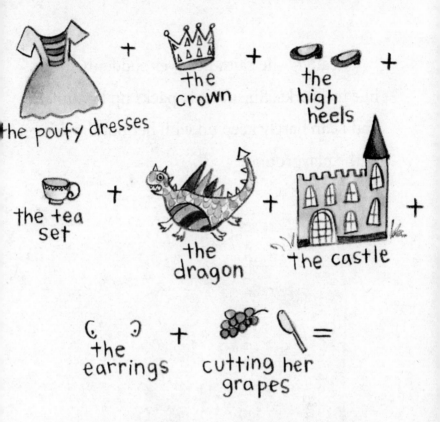

the poufy dresses + the crown + the high heels +

the tea set + the dragon + the castle +

the earrings + cutting her grapes =

"No problem!" I say, smiling, because I'm certain that *Rosabelle is going to love this game!* I hang up. "Meet me on the playground," I say to Rosabelle in my dead serious voice. "You're in danger and it's top secret."

"Really?" she says, her eyes suddenly lit up like fireworks. She quickly packs up her lunch and I can barely keep up with her out the door to the playground.

Rosabelle screams SOOOOO LOUD when
I tell her about Mrs. Gobble Gracker that the
hopscotch girls cover their ears and run away.

"Tell me everything," says Rosabelle. "And I mean *everything*."

"Well, she has pointy teeth, a black cape, a long nose, sharp black nails, crooked shoes, a creepy bun ...

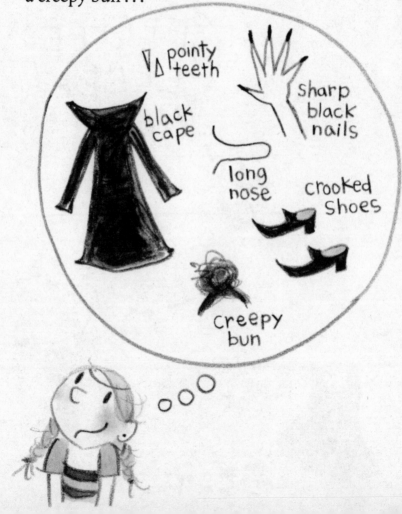

Rosabelle walks back and forth, thinking. She looks very serious. For a long time, she doesn't say anything.

Finally, she opens her mouth to speak.

"We'll have to go to war," she says.

"*War???*" I say.

"Do you have a horse?"

"Um . . ."

"*You need a horse!* We have to be prepared to fight. This war isn't just about us. This is about protecting the whole kingdom. Who else is on Mrs. Gobble Gracker's side?"

"I don't think anybody. . . . I've never seen anyone else but . . ."

"She is definitely not working alone! I'm sure she has helpers. How many prisoners has she already taken? And where are they all?" asks Rosabelle.

"Um . . . um . . . I don't know . . . ," I say. "I never thought about it. She has a cave."

"*You never thought about it??*" Rosabelle

gasps. "This is about injustice! We'll have to free them! I bet her cave is *full* of prisoners! It's up to US to save them! We need a plan. A *real plan*. We can't take any risks. I'm not going to spend the rest of my life spinning gold in a cave, or whatever!"

Then she starts talking even faster. "It's too bad my dragon is so injured right now, but I can gather some knights when I get home from school . . .

"and we need to make
a map of the woods
to locate her cave,

and I'll get my horse . . .

and see if I can find my
sword . . . and . . .

. . . and . . . lemon juice!"
she suddenly shouts. "We'll
need your lemon juice!"

And then recess is over.

That afternoon during math time, I whisper to Rosabelle, "There's one more thing I have to tell you. I have a fairy godmother named Mr. Nuggy, and he accidentally turned into a chicken."

"Oh! That same thing happened to my fairy godmother once!" whispers Rosabelle.

"Hey! What are you guys talking about?" asks George. "Chicken? Raise your hand if you love chicken!"

That night at dinner, my dad asks me, "Dory, what happened at school today?"

"Rosabelle and I planned a war!" I shout.

"Thank God it's Friday," says my mom.

Friday Night

Peter Pan hat

my goggles

Captain America Shield

Horsey

flashlight and large fork

backpack full of bananas

Luke's army pants

MARY, READY FOR WAR

CHAPTER 6
In the Woods

It's Saturday morning and I just want to stay home in my nightgown, but my dad drags us to the park.

As soon as we get there, I hang on my dad and whine, "Can we go home now?"

"No," he says. "Go play."

Instead, I ask him questions. Any question I can think of.

"Can't you just go on the swings?" asks my dad.

I wait for the swings. And wait. And wait. And wait. Every time I'm about to get a swing, a big kid races up and gets it before me.

Ugh! Big kids.

I guess I'll go dig in the sandbox. But right away I dig to the bottom. I hit wood. "I guess there's nowhere left to go," I grumble.

Next, I try to go down the slide, but this giant toddler with a gross runny nose keeps running up the slide.

"Can you move, please?" I ask him a million times. "MOVE! Or you are going to get hit when I go down!"

After a couple of times crashing into him face-to-face, I worry that I could catch his runny nose. Yuck. Forget this slide.

Luke is running around chasing pigeons with a stick. And Violet is with her friends. Violet always has friends at the park.

"*Now* can we go home?" I ask my dad. But he's reading a book and not listening to me.

That's when I see a chicken over there by that tree. I crawl to the other side of the bench to get a better look.

"Hey, Dad, I'm going to play right near those trees over there," I say.

"Okay," he says. "Don't go too far."

I'm really good at pretending I'm far away, when I'm not.

"Mr. Nuggy! Are you okay?" I say, picking up the chicken and kissing him. *He's soooooo cute as a chicken!*

"Bok!" he says.

"How did you get free?" I ask. But it's true, all he can do is bok.

"How do I turn you back into my fairy god-mother?"

"Bok! Bok!"

"Right! You need your magic wand! Where is it?"

He points deep into the woods.

"Okay," I say, "let's go find it."

We walk through the woods for hours.

Along the way,
many animals
stop to greet us.

Then I see a mysterious girl coming toward me through the woods. She is wearing a long fancy dress with a tall pointy hat with ribbons hanging down. As she gets closer, I see that she is carrying a wooden sword and eating an apple.

It's Rosabelle.

When she sees me, she smiles for a second and then she starts screaming, "Help! Help! This apple is poisonous. I'm slowly dying!" And then she falls to the ground.

"I'm dying, I'm dying," she says, and makes lots of creepy dying sounds. "Uuugg-hhhh, Eeee-uuu . . ."

"Who gave you the apple?" I ask.

"Kkk-hhhhggg . . . a very old woman," she says in a weak voice I can barely hear. Her eyes are closed.

"What did she look like?" I ask.

"She had a black bun, a big collar, and evil eyebrows. She had teeth as sharp as scissors . . . a nose as long as a broomstick . . . a cape as dark as midnight."

I try to imagine who this could be.

And then I realize, "Stupid me! You mean *Mrs. Gobble Gracker!*"

"Yes, her," Rosabelle says. "I was on my way to my cottage in the woods, and my dragon was so tired he fell asleep under a tree, and I was all alone, and suddenly I was caught in this big horrible net! Mrs. Gobble Gracker's trap!"

"Of course!" I say, remembering that Mrs. Gobble Gracker wanted a princess. "She captured you! That explains why she freed Mr. Nuggy!"

"Anyway," says Rosabelle, "she seemed a little nice at first, because she offered me this apple. It looked so red and juicy, but as soon as I took a tiny bite, I started to feel my ears getting hot, my toes very itchy, and my heart was *sweating*! And I knew right away that I WAS DYING."

"Wow! Mrs. Gobble Gracker is deadlier than I thought!" I say. "How did she make a poison apple spell?"

That's when Mr. Nuggy starts bokking his head off, flapping his wings, and getting all big and puffy. He is trying to tell me something.

He boks so hard he actually throws up.

Poor guy.

And then I suddenly figure out what he is trying to tell me.

"*Because she stole your magic wand! That's how!!*" I yell.

"BOK!" he says, jumping back onto his feet.

"How did she get your wand?" I ask.

"Bok! Bok!"

"Because you're a chicken and you have no hands or cool belt holder anymore?"

"BOK!"

"Awwww, it's okay. I'll get it back," I say petting him.

"Come on, we've got to go," I tell Rosabelle. "I can reverse the spell, but I'll need the magic wand. And the only way to get it is to battle Mrs. Gobble Gracker for it. We've got to find her cave!"

In her weak voice, Rosabelle says, "We don't have a lot of time."

"I know you're dying, but can you get up?"

"Can you come with me? Can you walk a little?"

"Just a little," she says, barely able to breathe.

And that's when we discover Mrs. Gobble Gracker's footprints.

CHAPTER 7
Launched into Battle

We follow Mrs. Gobble Gracker's pointy footprints into a creepy bat cave, through a giant spiderweb, and into a thick dark forest. . . .

I clear a path through the forest by chopping down little trees and branches with Rosabelle's sword.

On the other side of the forest, we find Mrs. Gobble Gracker sitting by a fire. From behind the bushes, Rosabelle waves quietly to the prisoners who are peeking out of the cave.

"What should we do now?" I whisper to Rosabelle.

"Well, I'm dying," she whispers. "So, YOU jump out with the sword."

"I need to look scary," I say.

"That's easy," she says.

Behind the bushes, Rosabelle rubs some mud on my face and arms.

"How about this?" I whisper, putting my shirt over my head, which makes my hair stick straight up.

"How about this?" she says, and then mushes up my hair even more and throws a bunch of pine needles in it.

"Now you look like a super freak!" she laughs. "Come here, I'll launch you."

I've never been launched before!

"Wait. Just in case we need it, I've got lemon juice," Rosabelle says.

Then she ducks down low and pushes me in the butt, hard.

I'M LAUNCHED!

I land on my feet.

"Dory?" says Mrs. Gobble Gracker. "Is that you?"

"Nope," I say, shaking my head. "Not me."

I forgot how easy it is to trick her.

"Well, whoever you are, did you come for Violet's doll?"

"Nobody cares about that doll anymore. Not even Violet. I came for the wand," I say.

"Ha-ha! Good luck with that!" she says.

Mrs. Gobble Gracker pulls out her own sword. Bigger, shinier, and sharper.

But with one ninja slash from me, and a squirt of lemon juice in the eye from Rosabelle, Mrs. Gobble Gracker is blinded and her cape catches on fire.

"Remember when I asked you
if she has helpers?" says Rosabelle,
clenching her teeth.

Rosabelle's dragon leads the knights to our rescue and together we fight a wild and crazy battle.

And lose.

But nobody thought to tie up a chicken.

Mr. Nuggy runs into the cave . . .

grabs the wand and . . .

chicken no more.

Mr. Nuggy quickly unties us and then frees the prisoners.

After our escape, everyone runs home, except us. Now that Mr. Nuggy is finally back to himself, we laugh really hard that he was a chicken. Hilarious!

Then Mr. Nuggy reverses Rosabelle's poison spell.

"Now hop around on one foot, and sneeze two times, and bend your elbows back like this," he tells her.

"How can I hop around on one foot when I'm dying? Okay, fine!" says Rosabelle. "And by the way, nice hat."

"You too," he says.

As soon as the spell is reversed, Rosabelle says, "Uh-oh. Did you hear a noise? Listen!"

I hear Violet calling me from the playground. "Rascal! Come on! We're leaving! It's starting to rain."

"Oh no!" I say. "I wish we were still tied up."

"I know," says Rosabelle, wiping dirt off my face. "But we better go."

We say good-bye to Mr. Nuggy, since he lives in the woods anyway. Before he leaves, he whispers to me, "The pancake recipe was too complicated. I can't . . ."

"It's okay," I say. "School's not THAT bad."

"It was nice to meet you," Rosabelle says to Mr. Nuggy.

Rosabelle and I walk back into the playground.

"This is my best friend, Rosabelle," I say, introducing her to Luke and Violet.

Their mouths drop open in disbelief.

"Huh???" says Luke.

"*Rosabelle??*" says Violet.

"Rosabelle, come on! We're leaving, too."

"I'm coming, Daddy!" calls Rosabelle.

Her dad definitely does not look like a king.

"Bye, Rascal!" waves Rosabelle. "See you on Monday!!"

Luke and Violet stare at Rosabelle as she walks off holding her daddy's hand.

Then they look at me.

"Told you," I say.

"And then what happened?" asks Mary.

"After the princess was saved from Mrs. Gobble Gracker's spell, all the creatures in the woods cheered with joy," I say. "The prisoners went home to their mushroom houses. The woods was a peaceful place again. And I was a hero."

"Wow! Tell it again," says Mary.

The End

Follow Dory and her outrageous
imagination on another adventure.
Turn the page for an excerpt from

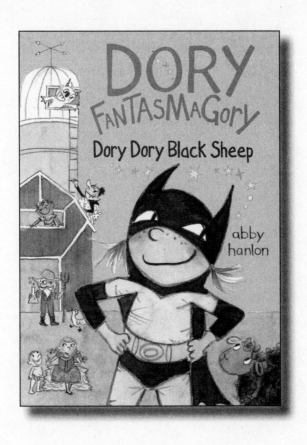

CHAPTER 1
Such a Baby Book

My name is Dory, but everyone calls me Rascal. I am six. I have a lot of freckles. My hair is messy. This is my nightgown that I try to wear as much as I can.

But the most important thing about me is that I have two worlds. One is real and one is imaginary.

This is my real world:

Mom and Dad

Big brother, Luke

Big sister Violet

Brand new best friend Rosabelle

Old friend George

This is my imaginary world:

My two worlds swirl together like a chocolate and vanilla ice-cream cone. Real and unreal get all mixed up into one crazy flavor. And a LOT of things happen to me. But my brother and sister just say I'm annoying. And they say I eat gross.

Every morning, Luke and Violet build a wall of cereal boxes around me so they can't see me eat.

"I just can't watch her slurping up her soggy cereal," says Luke.

"I just can't look at the milk dipping down her chin," says Violet. *"Augck!"*

But I'm not listening to them. Because Mrs. Gobble Gracker is on the back of my cereal box. I don't know what it says, but I can tell it's bad news.

Then my mom comes in the kitchen and starts screaming her head off.

RASCAL! YOU AREN'T DRESSED YET?

But before I get dressed, I have to wake up Mary. Lately, I've had to wake her up with a pan in my hand so she knows *I really mean it*. She's gotten super lazy now that she stays home when I'm at school.

I try to think of things that Mary can do when I'm gone.

Can you make 150 wet toilet-paper balls and put them under Violet's bed?

I don't want
her to feel left out.

You can
use Violet's
toothbrush...

At least she's happy when I brush her fur.

Stay
still.

Ouch!

Don't
stop.

On the walk to school, I invent a new game. It's called "Don't step on the Sticky Poij!" The Poij is poisonous gum. And if you step on it, it drains the blood out of your heart.

"It's everywhere! It's moving! It's alive!"

"You stepped on it!" I tell Luke.

"No, I didn't," says Luke.

"It's on your shoe!"

"There's nothing there."

"Help! Help!" I scream. "My brother is los-ing blood." I jump on Violet.

"Get off of me!"

The Poij oozes down the sidewalk all the way to school.

But as soon as I see Rosabelle in the school-yard, I forget about the Poij.

Rosabelle has a big huge chapter book in her lap. She looks up and sees me running toward her.

We take turns picking each other up. It's like hugging, but more dangerous. It's fun to pick up Rosabelle because she is so poufy. She wears six skirts under her dress! She also wears a sparkly headband on her forehead, which she says is her crown. She has little tiny heels on her shoes that go *clickety-click* on the play-ground. Today she has flowers stuck in her headband that look like she made them out of tissue paper.

"I love pretending to read chapter books, too!" I say, and grab her book and open it. I say, "Now *this book* is great for kids but totally inappropriate for grown-ups. Kids, listen! Grown-ups, cover your ears!"

Rosabelle thinks I'm funny.

Then it's time to go inside.

I love my classroom because Rosabelle sits right next to me. On the other side of me is George. While Rosabelle is busy drawing, George asks lots of questions. . . .

"Raise your hand if you ever found a LEGO in your underwear," he says.

I raise my hand.

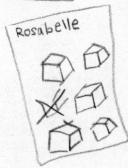

"Raise your hand if your mom ever told you to shut up!"

I raise my hand again.

"Raise your hand if you ever hurt your thumb dancing?"

Just George raises his hand.

"Raise your hand if . . ." but our teacher interrupts because it's time for morning meeting.